AMAZING
MACHINES
COLOSSAL
CRANES

To Rowan, from Grandpa Tony, with love x

Designed by Anthony Hannant (LittleRedAnt) 2021

Published in the United States by Kingfisher,
120 Broadway, New York, NY 10271
Kingfisher is an imprint of Macmillan Children's Books, London.

Distributed in the U.S. and Canada by Macmillan, 120 Broadway, New York, NY 10271

Library of Congress Cataloging-in-Publication data has been applied for

ISBN 978-0-7534-7653-6 (Hardback)
ISBN 978-0-7534-7651-2 (Paperback)

Kingfisher books are available for special promotions and premiums. For details contact:
Special Markets Department, Macmillan, 120 Broadway, New York, NY 10271

For more information, please visit
www.kingfisherbooks.com

Printed in China
9 8 7 6 5 4 3 2 1

COLOSSAL CRANES

Tony Mitton
and Ant Parker

KINGFISHER
LONDON & NEW YORK

5

Cranes are very powerful.
They tower way up high.
They help construct the buildings
that soar up to the sky.

And though there's something heavy
that's very hard to shift,
there won't be many things a crane
won't have the strength to lift.

A crane has got a tower
that gives it so much height.
Near the top a cab is placed.
It's almost out of sight.

An operator sits inside.
From way above the ground
the operator works controls
to move the crane around.

Above the cab's a main jib
with a trolley and a hook.
The hook can hoist up heavy loads
with steel cables—look!

Whoosh!

jib
trolley
hook
slewing gear

And when the load is lifted,
the crane can swing about
by circling on its slewing gear.
"That's good!" the ground crew shout.

Cranes aren't just for building.
They're good for loading too.

They load up train and ship containers.
See what they can do!

When buildings are too dangerous
and seem about to fall,

cranes can come and knock them down,
with a giant wrecking ball!

If workers need to work high up
on street lights or tall trees,

a crane can lift a bucket
that will get them there with ease.

This crane works on water.
It's carried by a barge.
A crane-on-boat that stays afloat?
Surely it's too large?

But no, it rescues sunken ships!
It's buoyant though it's big.
And now it's helping out at sea
to build an oil rig.

Gantry cranes are massive
and they move along on rails.

They'll build a ship or mend it,
until it hoots and sails.

Crawler cranes have caterpillar treads
and move along.

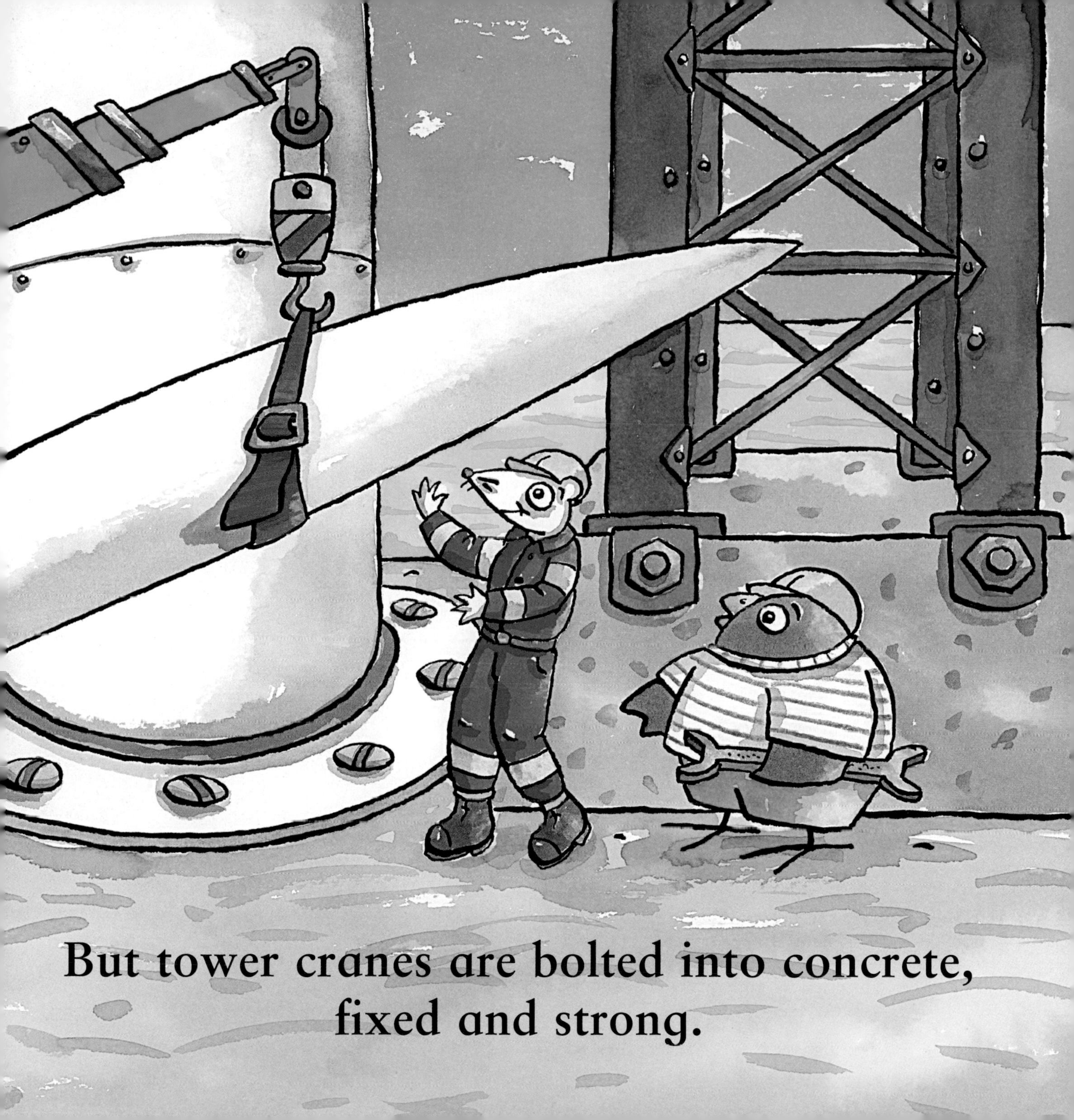

But tower cranes are bolted into concrete,
fixed and strong.

Once a building's finished
there's another job to start.
And so it's very handy that
a tower crane comes apart.

When it's all in pieces
it isn't like a crane . . .
and yet in just a day or two
it's back at work again!

Crane bits

jib
this is the working arm of the crane. It carries the load

trolley
this travels along the jib carrying the load in and out from the center of the crane

hook
this moves up and down to lift the load

bucket
this moves a worker up to fix things up high. It can also be attached to the hook to carry materials

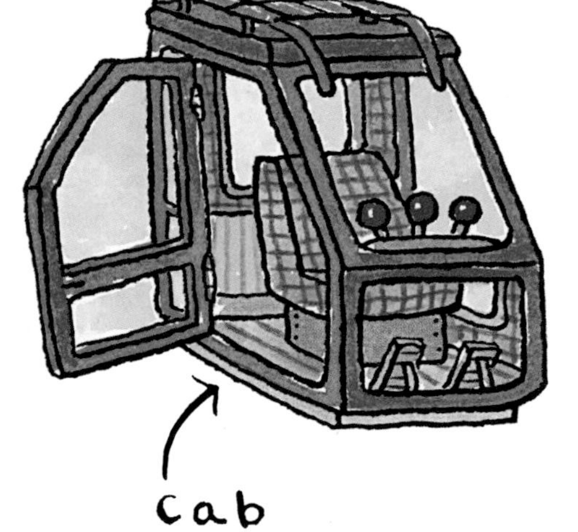

slewing gear
this is the crane's gear and motor, which allows the crane to spin around

cab
this is where the crane operator sits to control the crane's movements